An Easter Journey

Written by
Julia Zheng

Illustrated by
Alexandra Novoselskaya

First printing edition, 2022
Library of Congress Control Number: 2022917463
ISBN: 979-8-9869799-5-3

Printed in the United States of America

For my niece Candy and
nephew Leon, with love

Easter had arrived. Candy's mother told her to take a basket of Easter eggs to her grandma's house since she had to stay home to take care of her newborn baby.

Before Candy left, her mother reminded her, "Dear Candy, I decorated the eggs with colored pencils. Please remember not to get them wet, or they won't look pretty anymore!"

Candy nodded, and off she went.

On her way past the woods, Candy saw a turtle that was stuck in a mudhole. She picked up a stick from the road and pulled the turtle out.

"Thank you so much for your help!" the turtle said with a big smile.
"You are welcome. I'm glad I could help!" Candy answered happily.

As she continued on her path, Candy saw a frog with one leg caught in a fence. Candy went closer and helped the frog free his leg.

"Thank you so much for your help!" the frog said with a big smile.
"You are welcome. I'm glad I could help!" Candy answered happily.

Candy whistled as she walked. After a while, she saw a swan with her neck trapped in a net. Candy went ahead and freed the swan.

"Thank you so much for your help!" the swan said with a big smile. "You are welcome. I'm glad I could help!" Candy answered happily.

Candy kept walking. Soon, she came upon a river. "Oh, no! I can't swim. I have to keep these Easter eggs dry. What can I do?" Candy was worried.

Suddenly, a voice said, "Don't worry, my friend. I will give you a ride. Climb on my back and I will take you across the river."

Candy saw it was the turtle she helped earlier, and she climbed onto his back carefully. When Candy arrived at the other side of the river, she thanked the turtle.

Candy went on with her journey, until suddenly it started to rain. She covered the Easter eggs with her hand quickly and wondered what to do.

Then, a big shadow appeared above her head. When Candy looked around, she found that the frog she had helped earlier had covered her and her basket with a huge lotus leaf.

Candy thanked the frog, and they stayed under the lotus leaf together until the rain stopped.

Candy set off on her journey again and came across a waterfall. She was trying to figure out what to do when the swan she had saved earlier landed in front of her and offered her a ride.

Candy climbed up onto the swan's back quickly, and together they flew over the waterfall.

Candy thanked the swan and waved goodbye.

Finally, Candy arrived at her grandma's house. She rang the doorbell and her grandma opened the door.

"Happy Easter, Grandma!" said Candy as she handed over the Easter egg basket.

"Thank you, my sweet Candy. Come on in!" Candy's grandma was very happy to see her.

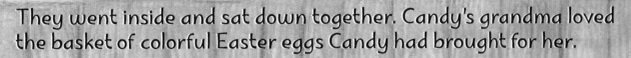

They went inside and sat down together. Candy's grandma loved the basket of colorful Easter eggs Candy had brought for her.

More importantly, she loved Candy's story of how she made her journey there without getting any of the Easter eggs wet with the help of her new friends!

About the Author

Julia Zheng is a children's author from Fujian, China. She now lives in Massachusetts. Zheng graduated from Nanchang University, where she majored in English and studied Western culture. She taught English in a primary school in southern China before moving to the United States. Her teaching experience and passion  for writing have inspired her to write children's books, filled with stories that convey important messages through humor, warmth, and a happy or unexpected ending.

For more books by Julia Zheng, please visit her Amazon Author Page:

https://www.amazon.com/author/juliazheng

Other books by Julia Zheng available on Amazon.com:

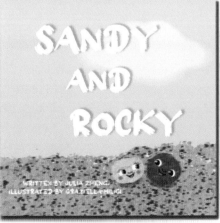

Printed in Great Britain
by Amazon

20479524R10016